This edition published in 1993 by Mimosa Books, distributed by Outlet Book Company, Inc., a Random House Company, 40 Engelhard Avenue, Avenel, New Jersey 07001.

2 4 6 8 10 9 7 5 3 1

First published in 1993 by Grisewood & Dempsey Ltd.
Copyright © Grisewood & Dempsey Ltd. 1993

ISBN 1 85698 518 0

Printed and bound in Italy

CINDERELLA

AND OTHER STORIES

MIMOSA
·BOOKS·

NEW YORK • AVENEL, NEW JERSEY

Cinderella

There was once a gentleman who lived in a fine house, with his kind and gentle wife and their pretty daughter. His wife died, so the gentleman married again. His new wife was not at all kind or pretty. She had been married before and had two daughters who were known, behind their backs, as the Ugly Sisters.

Although they had no reason to be unkind, the two sisters were horrid to their new stepsister. They ordered her about, scolded her and made her do all the work in the big house. Her clothes became ragged and thin and far too small. The poor girl was always cold and tired. In the evenings she would rest on a stool close to the fire, almost in the cinders and ashes.

"Cinderella. That's the perfect name for you," jeered the stepsisters when they saw her trying to keep warm.

Now the king and queen of their country had a son, and they planned a big ball for the prince in the hope that he might find a bride. Invitations were sent to all the big houses. When a large invitation card to the royal ball arrived at Cinderella's house, there was a great flurry of excitement. New dresses were chosen for the Ugly Sisters and their mother, and nobody talked about anything except the ball.

"I am sure the prince will fall in love with me," said one sister, smiling at herself in the mirror.

"You silly fool," said the other, pushing her aside. "He won't be able to resist falling in love with me. Just think, one day I could be queen," and she pretended she was the queen already as she ordered Cinderella to get another pair of shoes for her to try on. No one thought of asking Cinderella if she would like to go to the ball. They scarcely even noticed her as they rushed around trying on different wigs, fans, and gloves to go with their new ball dresses.

At last the day of the ball came, and Cinderella worked harder than ever, helping the Ugly Sisters and her stepmother to get ready. They quarreled with each other all day, and by the time

8

the carriage drove away to the king's palace, with all the family in it, Cinderella was glad to have some peace. But as she sat on her stool by the fire she could not help a tear falling onto the ashes, for she wished that she could have gone with them.

Suddenly she realized that she was not alone. A beautiful lady stood before her with a silver wand in her hand.

"Cinderella," she said, "I am your fairy godmother. Tell me, what are those tears for?"

Cinderella looked away.

"I wish, oh how I wish, I could have gone to the ball too."

"So you shall," said her fairy godmother, "but first we have some work to do. For if you are to go to the ball, I cannot send you as you are. Fetch me the largest pumpkin you can find in the garden."

Cinderella fetched the largest pumpkin she could see and with just a wave of her wand, her fairy godmother turned it into a gleaming golden coach.

"Now we need a few horses," said her godmother. "Look in the mouse trap and see if there is anything we can use."

Cinderella ran to the larder and found six mice running around in a cage. She watched her godmother wave her wand and suddenly, harnessed to the coach, there were six shining dappled horses, stamping their feet.

"Those horses need a coachman," decided her godmother. "Look in the rat trap, Cinderella." There were three rats in the trap and as the godmother touched the largest rat with her wand, it disappeared. But now up at the front of the coach sat a fine plump whiskery coachman in a smart uniform.

"Go and look behind the water barrel, Cinderella," said her godmother, "and see if you can find something we can use for footmen."

Cinderella ran to the water barrel and brought two lizards to her godmother. At the wave of her wand they were transformed into splendid footmen.

"There now, Cinderella, your coach is ready," said her godmother with a smile. "You will be able to go to the ball after all."

"How can I go like this?" sighed Cinderella, looking down in despair at her ragged clothes and bare feet. Her godmother touched her with her wand – her rags turned into a shimmering gown and on her feet she was wearing the prettiest pair of glass shoes she had ever seen.

As Cinderella stepped into the coach her godmother gave her a strict warning. "The magic will only last until midnight, and then everything will return to what it was before. Be sure you leave the ball before midnight, Cinderella."

When Cinderella's coach arrived at the palace the word went round that a beautiful lady had arrived in such a splendid coach that she must be a princess. The prince himself came down the steps to greet her and led her to the ballroom. As they entered, the other guests fell silent in wonder and the musicians stopped playing. The prince signaled to the musicians to play again and danced with Cinderella.

The prince stayed at Cinderella's side all evening. No one knew who she was. Not even the Ugly Sisters recognized her. Cinderella was so happy that she did not notice how quickly the time was flying by.

Suddenly she heard the clock strike the first stroke of midnight. With a cry she left the prince and ran out of the ballroom. As she flew down the steps, one of her shoes fell off, but she could not stop to pick it up.

Although the prince tried to follow Cinderella through the crowd, he soon lost sight of her. He questioned everyone carefully

but no one had seen the beautiful lady leave. The guards said that the only person who had gone out was a young raggedly-dressed girl. No one noticed the pumpkin in the corner of the courtyard or some mice, a rat and a pair of lizards that slunk into the shadows. But the prince did find the glass shoe on the steps, and he recognized it as one of the elegant shoes the mysterious and lovely lady had worn.

The next day the Ugly Sisters could talk of nothing but the beautiful lady who had captured the prince's heart and how she had disappeared so suddenly and how no one knew her name.

The palace issued a proclamation that the prince was looking for the lady who had worn the glass shoe. His servants would tour the country with it until they found the lady whose foot it fitted and the prince would marry that lady. The prince traveled around with his servants but time and again he was disappointed as the shoe failed to fit any lady's foot.

At last they came to Cinderella's house. The Ugly Sisters were waiting.

"Let me try first," cried one, holding out her foot, and pushing as hard as she could to squeeze it into the shoe. But it was no good. She gave up and laughed at her sister's efforts as she, too, tried to force her foot into the tiny glass shoe. When she had failed, Cinderella stepped forward.

"You!" sneered the Ugly Sisters. "But you were not even at the ball."

Cinderella slipped her foot into the glass shoe – it fitted perfectly. Then she drew from behind her back a second shoe which she put on her other foot. At the same moment the fairy godmother appeared and touched Cinderella with her wand. Instantly her ragged clothes changed back into the beautiful shimmering dress, and Cinderella once again became the lovely stranger.

The delighted prince asked Cinderella to marry him and Cinderella replied that there was nothing she would like more. The Ugly Sisters begged Cinderella to forgive them for their unkindness and she happily agreed. There was a fine royal wedding for Cinderella and the prince, and they lived happily ever after.

Cinderella found two husbands for the Ugly Sisters at court, and they too lived happily ever after – well, almost.

Country Mouse, Town Mouse

There was once a little mouse who lived very happily in the country. He ate grains of wheat and grass seeds, nibbled turnips in the fields, and had a safe snug house in a hedgerow. On sunny days he would curl up on the bank near his nest and warm himself, and in the winter he would scamper in the fields with his friends.

He was delighted when he heard his cousin from the town was coming to visit him, and fetched some of the best food from his store cupboard so he could share it with him. When his cousin arrived, he proudly offered him some fine grains of dried wheat and some particularly good nuts he had put away in the autumn.

His cousin, the town mouse, however, was not impressed. "You call this good food?" he asked. "My dear fellow, you must come and stay with me in the city. I will then show you what fine living is all about. Come with me tomorrow, for not a day should be lost before you see the excellent hospitality I can offer."

So the two mice traveled up to town. From his cousin's mousehole, the country mouse watched with wonder a grand dinner which the people who lived in the house were giving. He stared in amazement at the variety of cheese, the beautiful

14

vegetables, the fresh white rolls, the fruit, and the wine served from glittering decanters.

"Now's our chance," said the town mouse, as the dining-room emptied. The two mice came out of the hole, and scurried across the floor to where the crumbs lay scattered beneath the table. Never had the country mouse eaten such delicacies, or tasted such fine food. "My cousin was right," he thought as he nibbled at a fine juicy grape. "This is the good life!"

All of a sudden a great fierce furry beast leapt into the room and pounced on the mice.

"Run for it, little cousin!" shouted the town mouse, and together they reached the mousehole gasping for breath and shaking with fright. The cat settled down outside the hole, tail twitching, to wait for them.

"Don't worry. He will get bored soon, and go and amuse himself elsewhere. We can then go and finish our feast," said the town mouse.

"You can go out there again, if you like," said the country mouse. "I shall not. I am leaving tonight by the back door to return to my country home. I would rather gnaw a humble vegetable there than live here amidst these dangers."

So the country mouse lived happily in the country, the town mouse in the town. Each was content with the way of life he was used to, and had no desire to change.

The Selfish Giant

Every afternoon, as they were coming from school, the children used to go and play in the Giant's garden.

It was a large lovely garden, with soft green grass. Here and there over the grass stood beautiful flowers like stars, and there were twelve peach trees that in the springtime broke out into delicate blossoms of pink and pearl, and in the autumn bore rich fruit. The birds sat on the trees and sang so sweetly that the children used to stop their games in order to listen to them. "How happy we are here!" they cried to each other.

One day, the Giant came back. He had been to visit his friend the Cornish ogre, and had stayed with him for seven years. After the seven years were over he had said all that he had to say, for his conversation was limited, and he was determined to return to his own castle. When he arrived he saw the children playing in the garden.

"What are you doing here?" he cried in a very gruff voice, and the children ran away.

"My own garden is my own garden," said the Giant; "anyone can understand that, and I will allow nobody to play in it but myself." So he built a high wall all around it, and put up a noticeboard.

TRESPASSERS WILL BE PROSECUTED

He was a very selfish giant.

The poor children had nowhere to play. They tried to play in the road, but the road was very dusty and full of hard stones, and they did not like it. They used to wander around the high walls when their lessons were over, and talk about the beautiful garden inside. "How happy we were there!" they said to each other.

Then the Spring came, and all over the country there were little blossoms and little birds. Only in the garden of the Selfish Giant it was still winter. The birds did not care to sing in it as there were no children, and the trees forgot to blossom. Once a beautiful flower put its head out from the grass, but when it saw the notice-board it was so sorry for the children that it slipped back into the ground again and went off to sleep. The only people who were pleased were the Snow and the Frost.

"Spring has forgotten this garden," they cried, "so we will live here all the year round."

The Snow covered up the grass with her great white cloak, and the Frost painted all the trees silver. Then they invited the North Wind to stay with them, and he came. He was wrapped in furs, and he roared all day about the garden, and blew the chimney pots down. "This is a delightful spot," he said. "We must ask the Hail on a visit." So the Hail came. Every day for three hours he rattled on the roof of the castle till he broke most of the slates, and then ran round and round the garden as fast as he could. He was dressed in gray, and his breath was like ice.

"I cannot understand why the Spring is so late in coming," said the Selfish Giant, as he sat at the window and looked out at his cold, white garden; "I hope there will be a change in the weather."

But the Spring never came, nor the Summer. The Autumn gave golden fruit to every garden, but to the Giant's garden she gave

none. "He is too selfish," she said. So it was always winter there, and the North Wind and the Hail, and the Frost, and the Snow danced about through the trees.

One morning the Giant was lying awake in bed when he heard some lovely music. It sounded so sweet to his ears that he thought it must be the King's musicians passing by. It was really only a little linnet singing outside his window, but it was so long since he had heard a bird sing in his garden that it seemed to him to be the

most beautiful music in the world. Then the Hail stopped dancing over his head, and the North Wind stopped roaring, and a delicious perfume came to him through the open casement. "I believe the Spring has come at last," said the Giant; and he jumped out of bed and looked out.

What did he see?

He saw a most wonderful sight. Through a little hole in the wall the children had crept in, and they were sitting in the branches of the trees. In every tree that he could see there was a little child. And the trees were so glad to have the children back again that they had covered themselves with blossom, and were waving their arms gently above the children's heads. The birds were flying about and twittering with delight, and the flowers were looking up through the green grass and laughing.

It was a lovely scene, only in one corner was it still winter. It was the farthest corner of the garden, and in it was standing a

19

little boy. He was so small that he could not reach up to the branches of the tree, and he was wandering all around it, crying bitterly. The poor tree was still covered with frost and snow, and the North Wind was blowing and roaring above it. "Climb up! little boy," said the Tree, and it bent its branches down as low as it could: but the boy was too tiny.

And the Giant's heart melted as he looked out. "How selfish I have been!" he said; "now I know why the Spring would not come here. I will put that little boy on the top of the tree, and then I will knock down the wall, and my garden shall be the children's playground for ever and ever." He was really very sorry for what he had done.

So he crept downstairs and opened the front door quite softly, and went out into the garden. But when the children saw him they were so frightened that they all ran away, and the garden became winter again. Only the little boy did not run, for his eyes were so full of tears that he did not see the Giant coming. And the Giant stole up behind him and took him gently in his hand, and put him up into the tree. And the tree broke at once into blossom, and the birds came and sang on it, and the little boy stretched out his two arms and flung them around the Giant's neck, and kissed him. And the other children when they saw that the Giant was not wicked any longer, came running back, and with them came the Spring. "It is your garden now, little children," said the Giant, and he took a great ax and knocked down the wall. And when the people were going to market at twelve o'clock they found the giant playing with the children in the most beautiful garden they had ever seen.

All day long they played, and in the evening the children came to the Giant to bid him good-bye.

"But where is your little companion?" he said, "the boy I put into the tree." The Giant loved him best because he had kissed him.

"We don't know," answered the children: "he has gone away."

"You must tell him to be sure and come tomorrow," said the Giant. But the children said that they did not know where he lived, and had never seen him before; and the Giant felt very sad.

Every afternoon, when school was over, the children played with the Giant. But the little boy whom the Giant loved was never seen again. The Giant was very kind to all the children, yet he longed for his first little friend, and often spoke of him. "How I would like to see him!" he used to say.

Years went over, and the Giant grew very old and feeble. He could not play about any more, so he sat in a huge armchair, and watched the children at their games, and admired his garden. "I have many beautiful flowers," he said; "but the children are the most beautiful flowers of all."

One winter morning he looked out of his window as he was dressing. He did not hate the Winter now, for he knew it was merely the Spring asleep, and that the flowers were resting.

Suddenly he rubbed his eyes in wonder and looked and looked. It certainly was a marvelous sight. In the farthest corner of the garden was a tree quite covered with lovely white blossoms. Its branches were golden, and silver fruit hung down from them, and underneath it stood the little boy he had loved.

Downstairs ran the Giant in great joy, and out into the garden. He hastened across the grass, and came near to the child. And when he came quite close his face grew red with anger, and he said, "Who hath dared to wound thee?" For on the palms of the

22

child's hands were the prints of two nails, and the prints of two nails were on the little feet.

"Who hath dared to wound thee?" cried the Giant; "tell me that I may take my big sword and slay him."

"Nay," answered the child: "but these are the wounds of Love."

"Who art thou?" said the Giant, and a strange awe fell on him and he knelt before the little child.

And the child smiled on the Giant, and said to him, "You let me play once in your garden, today you shall come with me to my garden, which is Paradise."

And when the children ran in that afternoon, they found the Giant lying dead under the tree, all covered with white blossoms.

The Three Wishes

One day a poor woodcutter was working in the forest chopping down trees and sawing them into logs. He stopped for a moment and saw a fairy sitting on a leaf nearby.

"I have come," she told him, "to give you three wishes. The next three wishes you make will come true. Use them wisely."

After work, the woodcutter returned home and told his wife what had happened. She did not believe a word he said.

"You've just dreamed it," she laughed. "Still, just in case, you'd better think carefully before you wish."

Together they wondered. Should they wish for gold, jewels, a fine home? They argued and disagreed about everything until the woodcutter shouted crossly,

"I'm hungry after all my work. Let's eat first."

"I'm afraid there's only soup," his wife replied. "I'd no money to buy any meat."

"Soup again!" grumbled the woodcutter. "How I wish that we had a fine fat sausage to eat tonight."

Before they could blink, a fine fat sausage appeared on their kitchen table.

"You idiot!" screeched his wife. "Now you've wasted one of our precious wishes. You make me so angry." She went on scolding until he could stand it no more and he shouted,

"I wish that sausage was on the end of your nose!"

Immediately the large sausage jumped in the air and attached itself to the wife's nose. There she stood with the big fat sausage hanging down in front of her. It was difficult to talk with it hanging there and she became really angry when the woodcutter laughed at her because she looked so ridiculous. She pulled and pulled; he pulled and pulled. But the sausage stayed there, stuck on the end of her nose.

The woodcutter soon stopped laughing when he remembered they only had one of the fairy's wishes left.

"Let's wish," he said quickly, "for all the riches in the world."

"What good would that do," she asked, "with a long sausage hanging from my nose? I could not enjoy them for a minute!"

The woodcutter and his wife finally agreed that they could do nothing except get rid of that sausage-nose.

The woodcutter wished and in a flash the sausage was gone, and he and his wife sat down to eat the soup that she had prepared for their supper. The only point they could agree on for a long while was how foolish they had both been to use the fairy's wishes so unwisely. They also wished – too late by now – that they had eaten the sausage when it had first appeared.